D1503698

Published by Modern Publishing
A Division of Unisystems, Inc.,
under License by Joseph A. Marino Design Associates.

Copyright © 1987 Modern Publishing, a Division of Unisystems, Inc. and
Joseph A. Marino Design Associates.

® - Scrambled Eggs is a trademark owned by Joseph A. Marino.
and is registered in the U.S. Patent and Trademark Office.
Scrambled Egg Characters © 1987 Joseph A. Marino Design Associates.

® - Honey Bear Books is a trademark owned by Honey Bear Productions, Inc.,
and is registered in the U.S. Patent and Trademark Office.

No part of this book may be reproduced or copied without permission from the
publisher.

All Rights Reserved.

Printed in Singapore

THE CLUBHOUSE BUNNY

Written and Illustrated by Susan Marino

MODERN PUBLISHING
A Division of Unisystems, Inc.
New York, New York 10022

"Tag! You're it, Sunny," Egg Salad called as she tagged her brother and ran into the bushes to escape.

Sunny Side Up stopped dead in his tracks. Egg Salad was nowhere in sight. But his little brother, Egg Nog, peeked out from behind a nearby tree. "I'm going to get you," Sunny Side Up shouted as he dashed after him.

Sunny Side Up and Egg Nog toppled to the ground. They were laughing aloud when Egg Salad's voice interrupted from behind the bushes.

"Hey, you guys, come here quick and look at this," Egg Salad called.

The brothers ran to join her. "A bunny!" Egg Nog exclaimed. "We found a bunny."

"*I found a bunny*," Egg Salad boasted. "And he's mine."

"Aw, come on, Sis," Sunny said. "Can't we share him too?"
"We'll help take care of him," Egg Nog added.
Egg Salad stroked the bunny. "Oh, all right," she said as she carefully picked up the bunny and they all headed home.

The three Scrambled Eggs were passing under the clubhouse when Hard Boiled, their older brother, and his friend, Over Easy, spotted them.

"What do you have there?" Hard Boiled called.

Egg Salad held out the bunny for them to see.
"Wow! A cute little rabbit," Over Easy exclaimed.
"What are you going to do with him?" asked Hard Boiled.
"We don't know yet," Egg Salad answered.

Later, the Scrambled Eggs held a meeting to decide if the bunny could stay in their clubhouse.

"Please let us keep him here," Egg Salad begged.

"We'll watch after him," Sunny Side Up added.

Hard Boiled thought very carefully. "All right," he said at last. "The bunny can stay in the clubhouse as long as you take good care of him."

"We will, we will!" the younger Scrambled Eggs cheered.

The bunny was the little Scrambled Eggs' favorite friend. They named him Fuzzy because he was so soft and furry.

Sunny Side Up, Egg Salad and Egg Nog took turns tending to Fuzzy and everything worked out just fine until one day in May.

It was just about noon. Hard Boiled climbed the ladder to the clubhouse. He had his lunch and a bottle of water with him. He put his things down and peered into Fuzzy's box.

Fuzzy's food dish and water bowl were both empty.
"Oh, you poor bunny," Hard Boiled said. "You must be starving."
Hard Boiled went to work right away. He filled the water bowl
and put it under the bunny's nose. Fuzzy sipped and sipped. Then
he pinched a piece of lettuce from his own sandwich and held it
out for Fuzzy to eat. The bunny nibbled and nibbled. Soon Fuzzy
was full.

"That's better," Hard Boiled said as he stroked the bunny's fur. "Now you're coming with me because I've got a wonderful surprise for you."

Hard Boiled took Fuzzy and went back to the place where Egg Salad had found him.

"I think you'll be better off on your own," he said as he put Fuzzy on the ground. Fuzzy blinked, almost as if he were smiling. Then he turned toward the deep woods and hopped away.

When Hard Boiled returned to the clubhouse, Egg Salad was crying and the other Scrambled Eggs were very sad.

"There's nothing to cry about, Egg Salad," Hard Boiled said. "I'll tell you what happened."

As they listened, the other Scrambled Eggs looked at one another. "We said we would take care of Fuzzy," Egg Salad said.

"But I guess we didn't do a very good job," Egg Nog added.

Hard Boiled put his arms around the Scrambled Eggs. "I said there's nothing to be upset about because Fuzzy is very happy now."

The little Scrambled Eggs smiled. "And that makes us happy, too." they said.